SECOND-GRADE
PIG PALS

SECOND-GRADE PIG PALS

Kirby Larson

drawings by Nancy Poydar

Holiday House/New York

Library of Congress Cataloging-in-Publication Data
Larson, Kirby.
Second-grade pig pals / Kirby Larson ; drawings by Nancy Poydar.
—1st ed.
p. cm.
Summary: Second grader Quinn tries to earn a gold star on the
bulletin board for National Pig Day and regain her friendship
with a new student following a mix-up.
ISBN 0-8234-1107-9
[1. Friendship—Fiction. 2. Schools—Fiction.] I. Poydar,
Nancy, ill. II. Title.
PZ7.L32394Se   1994   93-16061   CIP   AC
[Fic]—dc20

CHAPTER ONE

"Mom, can I buy this for Mrs. Palmer?" Quinn Kelley held up a pink pencil with a pig eraser on top.

"*May I*," corrected her mother.

Quinn sighed. "May I buy this pencil for Mrs. Palmer?"

"Not today," Mom said. "You already owe me two dollars."

"But it's for school," Quinn said. "We're going to celebrate National Pig Day. Everyone in class is bringing things for the Pig Patch."

"Pig Patch?"

"Uh-huh. We fixed up the reading corner. We made a fence out of cardboard, and the rug is a pretend mud puddle—pigs love mud! Mrs. Palmer put a bookshelf right in the middle to hold the things people bring in."

"Oh, I see." Her mother smiled. "Kind of a hog heaven!"

Quinn nodded. "It's so neat, Mom. Rachel brought in pig cookies, with red hots for eyes. Cody's dad made him a little pom-pom pig. And Josh might get to bring in a real pig, if his mom says okay."

"That sounds like lots of fun." Her mother picked up another birthday card. "What about this one for Grandma?"

Quinn wrote her name in the air with the pig pencil. "How come you get to buy something and I don't?"

"You got to buy that new stationery with the monkeys on it. When you pay me back for that, you can save up for something else."

Quinn turned the pencil over in her palm. There was red writing on the side. It said PIG POWER.

"What if I sweep the driveway when I get home?" she asked.

"That would be worth fifty cents," her mother said. She got an envelope for the birthday card for Grandma. "Then you would only owe me one dollar and fifty cents."

Mom walked toward the cash register.

Quinn put the pig pencil carefully back on the display. It cost one dollar and twenty-nine cents. She did not even have the twenty-nine cents. She slowly carried the small white sack with Grandma's card in it to the car.

"Please hurry up. I still have to start dinner," said Mom, unlocking the car door.

Quinn got in and buckled her seat belt. She sniffled once or twice. She made small sad sounds in the front seat.

Her mother sighed. "I have an idea. How about making Mrs. Palmer a pig bookmark? We must have pink construction paper at home."

Quinn twisted her hair around her finger as she thought. No one had brought in a pig bookmark. And Mrs. Palmer was crazy about reading. But bossy old Annie May would probably say a bookmark was boring.

"It would just tear," said Quinn.

"Not if you cover it with plastic. I'll help you."

"Okay." Quinn decided she'd give her pig blue eyes, just like the pig pencil at the store.

When they got home, Quinn helped put away groceries. Then she found a piece of pink construction paper. It was only a little bit wrinkled. She drew a pig for Mrs. Palmer.

"What's that?" Quinn's big brother Tyson looked over her shoulder. He was all sweaty from basketball practice.

4

"P-U!" Quinn pushed him away.

"Is that a rabbit?" Tyson asked.

"No." Quinn hunched over her picture so he couldn't see.

"It's a horse."

"No." Quinn put her face down on her arms.

"A rhinoceros?"

"Tyson!" said Mom. "Go wash up, now. Dad will be home soon."

Quinn kept her face down so no one would see her watery eyes. Tyson was right. Her pig didn't look anything like a pig. It didn't even look like an animal. It looked like a pink dumpling. With blue eyes.

Quinn wadded up the paper. She threw it in the recycling bin.

Then she went to her room and made a sign. KEEP OUT!! She taped the sign to her bedroom door.

She sat on the floor and held Chi-Chi, her stuffed monkey. It felt good to squeeze him tight and rub his soft tail across her cheek. "I am the only one in the whole class who hasn't brought something for our Pig Patch. Even Cody did, and he never remembers anything."

Quinn looked around her room. She could understand about Mrs. Palmer liking pig things. Quinn had many monkey things. She had a T-shirt with monkeys on it. Her favorite poster, the one over her dresser, showed a chimpanzee swinging by one arm. There was even that new monkey stationery in her desk.

There were monkeys everywhere she looked. But not one pig. Nothing she could take to put in the Pig Patch. She would be the only one without a gold star on the star chart. She wished she was back in first grade. Second grade was too hard.

CHAPTER TWO

There was a surprise in Room 3 the next morning.

A new girl stood in front by Mrs. Palmer.

"This is Manuela," Mrs. Palmer said. "She has moved here to Washington all the way from Michigan."

"It's the 'mitten' state," Manuela told the class. On the wall map, Michigan did look like a mitten.

Quinn thought Manuela must be very

smart to be able to find Michigan on the map.

"And, in the winter, we wear our mittens!" Manuela smiled when she said that. She had a beautiful smile. Her four front permanent teeth had already grown in.

Quinn had two big holes on either side of her front teeth.

"I hate my holes," she told Manuela at lunch.

"Oh, I miss mine," Manuela said. "A straw used to fit right through them."

Quinn tried it out. The straw did fit just right. Her milk carton was empty in no time. "I'm going to do it again tomorrow."

"You're so lucky," Manuela said.

"I guess I am," Quinn agreed.

Mrs. Palmer stopped by Quinn's desk. "Would you show Manuela around the school before recess?"

Quinn sat up very tall. "Okay!" She and

Manuela quickly finished their lunches.

When they got outside, Manuela hugged herself. "I was so nervous about today," she said, smiling her beautiful smile.

"You were? How come?"

Manuela balanced on one leg. "I didn't know if anyone would like me. But then when you were so friendly at lunch, I felt lots better."

Quinn got a warm feeling inside. "I'm glad." She opened a door. "This is the main office. You have to come here if you're late or need a bus pass. To ride home with someone else or something."

Manuela nodded. "That's the way it was at my old school, too."

"And around here is the nurse's office. She's real nice. If you get a stomach-ache, she gives you a peppermint to suck on."

"Yum!" said Manuela. "The only thing I like better than peppermints is red lico-rice."

"I love red licorice, too. The fat ropes are

best," said Quinn. "Come on. We'll go see the principal. She gives out neat pencils to new kids."

Manuela looked nervous when she shook hands with Mrs. Moore.

"Glad to have you, Manuela. I bet Quinn is a wonderful guide."

"She is," answered Manuela.

Mrs. Moore got out a box of pencils. First, Manuela picked up a pink pencil. Then she picked up a yellow pencil.

"Are you looking for a special color?" asked Mrs. Moore.

"Purple. It's my favorite," said Manuela.

"It's mine, too!" said Quinn.

"Hmm. Let me see here." Mrs. Moore rummaged in her desk. "Here we go. Two purple pencils. One for each of you."

"Thank you." Quinn and Manuela answered at the same time. That made them giggle. They couldn't stop. Mrs. Moore smiled.

"Maybe it's time for you to go out for recess," she said.

They headed for the playfield.

"I can't believe we like so many of the same things," said Manuela. "What's your favorite book?"

"*Stone Fox*," said Quinn. "It made me cry."

"Me too!" exclaimed Manuela. "I like stories that make me cry. My favorite is *Anne of Green Gables*. I made my dad rent the video so many times that he bought it for me for my last birthday."

"I don't believe it." Quinn was amazed. "I love that movie, too. You're lucky to have your own copy."

"Would you like to watch it with me sometime?"

Before Quinn could answer, Annie May came running over.

"Quit hogging Manuela, Quinn. Come on, let's jump rope." Annie May grabbed Manuela and ran over to where Tiffany was waiting. They taught Manuela their rhyme.

"Cinderella dressed in yella,
Went upstairs to kiss her fella.
Kissed a snake by mistake.
How many doctors did it take?"

Annie May didn't miss until she got to thirty-five. Then Manuela taught them one of hers:

"Register, register, sign your name,
M-A-N-U-E-L-A.
First grade one, Second grade one, two
Third grade one, two, three . . ."

Manuela made it all the way to twelfth grade every time.

The girls jumped rope until the boys started chasing them. Then they all played soccer.

Manuela could run fast. In her red jacket, she was a red blur back and forth on the field.

At work stations, Manuela helped Quinn

with her spelling, and Quinn helped Manuela with math.

After school, they sat on the bus together.

"I never thought I'd find a best friend on my first day at this school," said Manuela. "Could you come over to my house tomorrow?"

Quinn felt like she would float away like a happy balloon. Manuela wanted her for a best friend! "I'll have to ask my mom," she said.

"Here." Manuela handed Quinn a scrap of paper. "It's my phone number. Call me and tell me if you can come."

Quinn held the paper carefully.

"No one has called me at our new house yet," said Manuela.

"I'll be the very first one."

The bus stopped. Manuela scooted off the seat.

"Tell your mother to say yes," she said.

When she got off the bus, she turned to wave at Quinn.

Quinn waved back. And kept waving until Manuela was just a red speck. She couldn't wait to get off at her own stop.

CHAPTER THREE

"Mom, Mom," Quinn called as soon as she was in the house.

"I'm in here," her mother answered from her office.

Quinn hurried down the hall to where her mother was working. "Can I go to Manuela's tomorrow after school?"

"It's 'May I?'," reminded Mom. "And who is Manuela?"

"She is a new girl. She lives near Tiffany

and Annie May. We are already best friends."

"That's great." Her mother stopped typing on her computer keyboard. "Going to Manuela's sounds fine, but not tomorrow."

"How come?"

"Tomorrow you have a dentist appointment."

"Can't you change it to another day?" Quinn hugged her mother's shoulders.

Quinn did not like the dentist. Her name was Dr. Walker. But she liked to be called Dr. Teeth.

Cody, who lived next door, was lucky. His dentist gave Frisbees and sugarless gumballs and glow-in-the-dark toothbrushes for treats. All Dr. Teeth ever gave was dental floss.

Quinn's mom hugged her back. "No, I can't change it. I've changed it twice already."

"But, Mom—"

"I'm sorry, honey. I'm sure there will be other days to go to Manuela's house."

Quinn dropped her bookbag with a thump. "But she gave me her phone number. She wants me to call and say yes."

Her mother began to type again. "Call and say yes you'd like to come. But another day. Now, why don't you go get a snack?"

Quinn stomped to the kitchen. She put the piece of paper with Manuela's phone number on the table. Now she did not want to call Manuela. She was scared to say she could not come.

Manuela might not wait until another day to have Quinn over to her house. She might ask Tiffany or Annie May instead. Then Quinn would not be the first person to go over to Manuela's. She would not be her best friend.

Quinn looked around. There were some apple slices and a graham cracker on a plate—a healthy snack again. Boring. She wished her mother bought Goody Cakes and Munchy Crunchies like Cody's mom did.

It wasn't fair. Not about snacks or dentists or not being able to go to Manuela's. But it was no good telling that to her mother. Mom would say, as she always did, that not everything in life was fair.

The piece of paper with Manuela's phone number still sat on the table. Quinn knew Manuela was waiting for her to call. But she just couldn't. What if Manuela didn't believe Quinn had a dentist appointment? She might think Quinn was making excuses, that she didn't want to come over at all. It would be easier to explain in person at school tomorrow.

Quinn took two apple slices and turned on the TV. She watched the whole Dizzy Duck show and didn't even smile once.

CHAPTER FOUR

The next morning, Quinn saved a seat for Manuela on the bus. She had two chocolate chip cookies wrapped in plastic just for her.

Manuela got on the bus with Annie May and Tiffany. "Come on, this way," said Annie May, tugging Manuela to the back of the bus. They walked right past Quinn's seat.

Quinn turned around to say "hi," but

some kids were in the way. She couldn't see Manuela.

"Manuela," Annie May said so the whole bus could hear, "my mom says I can have you and Tiffany over for a tea party. We get to have real tea. Can you come?"

Quinn didn't listen anymore. She put the cookies in her bookbag. She slumped down in the seat and closed her eyes.

She was the last one off the bus when they arrived at school.

She heard Manuela and Tiffany and Annie May giggling in the coatroom. They sounded like they were having fun.

At recess, Quinn played four square with them.

"You're out," called Annie May in her know-it-all voice.

"That was a liner," said Quinn.

"She's out, isn't she, Manuela?"

"Well, it looked like a liner to me," Manuela answered.

"Oh, who cares." Annie May threw down

the ball. "This is boring, anyway. Let's go play on the monkey bars." She grabbed Manuela's hand and they ran off.

"Want to play two square?" Tiffany asked Quinn.

"Okay. You can serve." Quinn got out right away because she was watching the monkey bars instead of the ball. She decided at lunchtime she would tell Manuela what had happened. She would tell her why she didn't call.

Quinn came back to her desk after buying lunch. Annie May was in her chair. Tiffany and Manuela and Jim and Josh were also sitting at Quinn's pod of desks.

"That's my chair," she said to Annie May.

"Mrs. Palmer said we could eat lunch here today." Annie May set a carton of yogurt on Quinn's desk. "You'll have to eat somewhere else."

Quinn took her tray and sat with Cody. His lunch was two Goody Cakes, a bag of chips, and a can of V8 juice.

"I packed my own lunch," he told Quinn proudly.

"It doesn't look very healthy," said Quinn.

"No, it doesn't," Cody said. His face was all smiles and marshmallow creme from the Goody Cakes. "Isn't it great?"

Quinn couldn't even eat the piece of Goody Cake Cody offered. She looked over at the kids by her desk and thought she saw Manuela give her a half-smile.

After lunch, Annie May made the daily report.

"This is Wednesday, February twenty-third," she said. She stood by Mrs. Palmer's desk. Her voice was loud and important. "Tomorrow will be Thurday, February twenty-fourth."

"And what shall we write in our class journal, Annie May?" Mrs. Palmer sat ready to write.

Annie May scrunched up her mouth and eyes. She looked around the room. Then she smiled.

"Write that *almost* everyone has a star on the Pig Patch chart," she said. She looked over at Quinn.

Tiffany spoke up. "Manuela doesn't count because she's new."

"Manuela can bring something later this week," said Mrs. Palmer.

"Well, everyone else has had plenty of time," Annie May said. She made snake eyes at Quinn.

Quinn bent over in her chair. She was sure everyone was staring at her. She pressed her hand against her stomach. How could Annie May be so mean?

"Let's write, 'Many people have brought in many interesting things for the Pig Patch,' " suggested Mrs. Palmer.

That made Quinn's stomach feel a little better. But not much.

She looked at Manuela. Manuela's face was pale and crumpled.

When Mrs. Palmer wasn't looking, Quinn made her ugliest face at Annie May.

Annie May's
hand shot
up in the
air to tattle.

"Please save
your comment
for later, Annie May,"
said Mrs. Palmer. "We
need to get on to our
spelling now."

Quinn sat back and
smiled a little smile.
So there, Annie May.

The good feelings did not last
for long. Nearly every word on the
spelling list had to do with pigs. There was
hoof and *oink* and *sow* and *corn* and *ham*.
It seemed like the blank spot next to
Quinn's name on the Pig Patch chart got
bigger and brighter with every word. The
bonus words were *squeal* and *snout*. By the
time the end-of-the-day bell rang, Quinn
felt worse than ever.

Her mother met her in front of the

school to take her to the dentist appointment. Quinn grumbled all the way there.

When Dr. Teeth gave her a purple tablet to chew, she barely moved her jaws up and down.

"She looks good, Mrs. Kelley," Dr. Teeth said as she used a mirror to check the very back of Quinn's mouth. "No cavities this time." Dr. Teeth lowered the chair so Quinn could hop out.

The lady at the desk gave Quinn a plain old toothbrush and a package of dental floss. The toothbrush was pink. Pig pink.

"They have glow-in-the-dark toothbrushes now," Quinn said.

"Hmm," said the lady at the desk.

"Really?" said Dr. Teeth. "Do you think I should get some?"

"Yes, I do," Quinn said.

"Then I better do that!" Dr. Teeth smiled.

Quinn wished that she had told her about the glow-in-the-dark toothbrushes a long time ago.

CHAPTER FIVE

Cody had lived next door to Quinn for so long that he did not bother to knock. He walked into the kitchen like he lived there.

"Just in time for a snack," said Quinn's mom. She sliced an orange for him.

"Mmm. Monster mouths. My favorite!" Cody put a wedge of orange over his teeth. He pulled his lips back.

"You're not a very scary monster," Quinn said. She put her head down on the table. She peeked up at him with one eye.

"Cody is too friendly to be a scary monster," said her mother. She lowered one eyebrow at Quinn. That was her "be nice" look.

Quinn sighed.

"Want to finish our fort?" asked Cody.

Before Quinn could say no, her mother answered,
"That sounds like fun. Would you like to take some supplies?"

"Like what?" Cody asked.

"All kinds of things," said Mom. "Like fairy sticks, and instant power pills, and magic tree bark."

"Wow!" said Cody.

31

"Don't get excited," Quinn said. "She just means string cheese and raisins and graham crackers."

"I still think it's a good idea," Cody said. "How about two bags of supplies, one for me and one for Quinn?"

"Sure," said Mom. She got two lunch sacks. She put a stick of string cheese, some raisins, and two graham crackers in each one.

Cody took the two sacks. "Come on," he said to Quinn. "I have to be home in half an hour."

Quinn followed him, slow as a slug, out to the fort.

"It's not a very good fort," she said. She poked at the big piece of plywood leaning against the stump. "It would fall down if a baby breathed on it."

"There aren't any babies around," Cody said. He got a stick and propped up the plywood. "It's the best fort on the block."

"Humph," said Quinn.

"Why are you so grumpy?" he asked.

Quinn didn't answer.

Cody turned his baseball cap around. "Annie May is a blabbermouth."

"I wish she'd blab her mouth right off." Quinn kicked the fort hard.

It started to wobble. Cody caught it and fixed everything right again. He slipped under the plywood and sat down in the fort.

"There's room for you," he said.

Quinn crawled in, too. The grass was soft. It was quiet and cozy.

"It's better once you are inside," she said to Cody.

He nodded. "I told you this is the best fort on the block."

Quinn ate a graham cracker.

"We did a good job building this," she said with her mouth full.

She peeked out from under the roof. "We had better watch out for dragons and spies," she said.

Cody picked up a twig. "My magic wand will protect us."

"Not from dragons *and* spies." Quinn looked for another twig. "We need two magic wands for that." She found one, too.

"Mine has stars on it," said Cody.

Stars reminded Quinn of the gold star she didn't have on the Pig Patch chart. "Mine doesn't. It has hearts. That's better."

Together they waved away a red-eyed fire breather named Orlock and a small, spiny dragon named Spike.

They turned one spy into a butterfly and one into a bowl of spinach. Another one got zapped into outer space.

"Our fort is the best fort *ever!*" said Cody.

"It is," said Quinn. Cody was fun to play with. He always made her laugh.

Cody rocked up on his knees. "Watch out! There's another one!"

With a swift sweep of her wand, Quinn turned the last spy into a monkey.

CHAPTER SIX

"I have something to share today." Mrs. Palmer pulled a huge green plastic bag out from under her desk. "Would you like to play Five Guesses?"

Everybody put thumbs up.

"Okay. Tiffany, what is your guess?"

"Is it a bag of balloons?"

Mrs. Palmer shook her head. "Jim?"

"Is it a sleeping bag?"

"No, not a sleeping bag. Cody?"

"Jim asked my question." Cody looked glum.

"Do you have another guess?"

"A pillow?"

"Not a pillow either. Two more guesses. Manuela, would you like to try?"

"Is it something to eat?" Manuela giggled.

Mrs. Palmer shook her head again. "Last guess. Annie May?"

"Is it something for our Pig Patch?"

"Good guess!" Mrs. Palmer smiled at Annie May.

Quinn scrunched up her face. Annie May was always lucky at guessing.

Everyone leaned forward to watch Annie May open the bag.

"A pig!" she cried. "A giant pig!"

Annie May squeezed the stuffed pig tight. "Oh, he's so soft."

Quinn waggled her hand in the air. So did Manuela. So did Tiffany and Jim and Cody. "Can we hold it, too?"

Mrs. Palmer clapped her hands to give

the quiet signal. Clap, clappa, clap, clap.

The children answered with a clap, clap. They knew it was time to settle down.

Mrs. Palmer nodded. "Let's pass the pig around. While you are waiting, you can be thinking. This pig needs a name. We are going to have a class contest to name our pig. Who-ever comes up with the name that gets the most votes will win a prize."

Quinn's feet did a hop-skip under her desk. Contests were exciting!

When it was Quinn's turn to hold the pig, she petted it carefully. Then she looked at its face. It had brown eyes and long curly eyelashes. It had a beautiful smile.

She gave the pig one last squeeze. Then she passed it on for someone else to have a turn.

All of a sudden, Quinn got a good feeling. She knew a beautiful name for their beautiful pig—a name that would win the contest *and* win back her best friend.

CHAPTER SEVEN

Mrs. Palmer passed out paper. "Write your suggestions down," she said. "Then we will vote on our favorite name."

Jim raised his hand. "Can this be a sloppy copy?"

"Great question. Use your good printing. If you aren't sure of spelling, let me know."

Quinn slowly wrote the letters of the name she was sure would win. It was hard. Her hand was so excited it wobbled a little.

She folded her paper in half very carefully.

She looked over at Manuela. She had finished, too.

Finally, everyone was finished.

Cody and Annie May were helpers of the day. They gathered up the papers and took turns reading.

"Buster," Cody read.

Then Annie May read, "Wilbur." She giggled. "That's mine," she said. "Like in *Charlotte's Web*."

Mrs. Palmer smiled at Annie May.

Cody unfolded another one. "Raspberry."

"Silent *p*," said Mrs. Palmer. "Like razzberry."

Tiffany sat up straighter and wiggled. Everybody knew that Raspberry was her name.

"Here are three that say Oinker." Cody flipped through the papers.

Mrs. Palmer wrote Oinker on the board.

Royce and Jim and Josh did high fives.

"This one says Hammy—" Cody started.

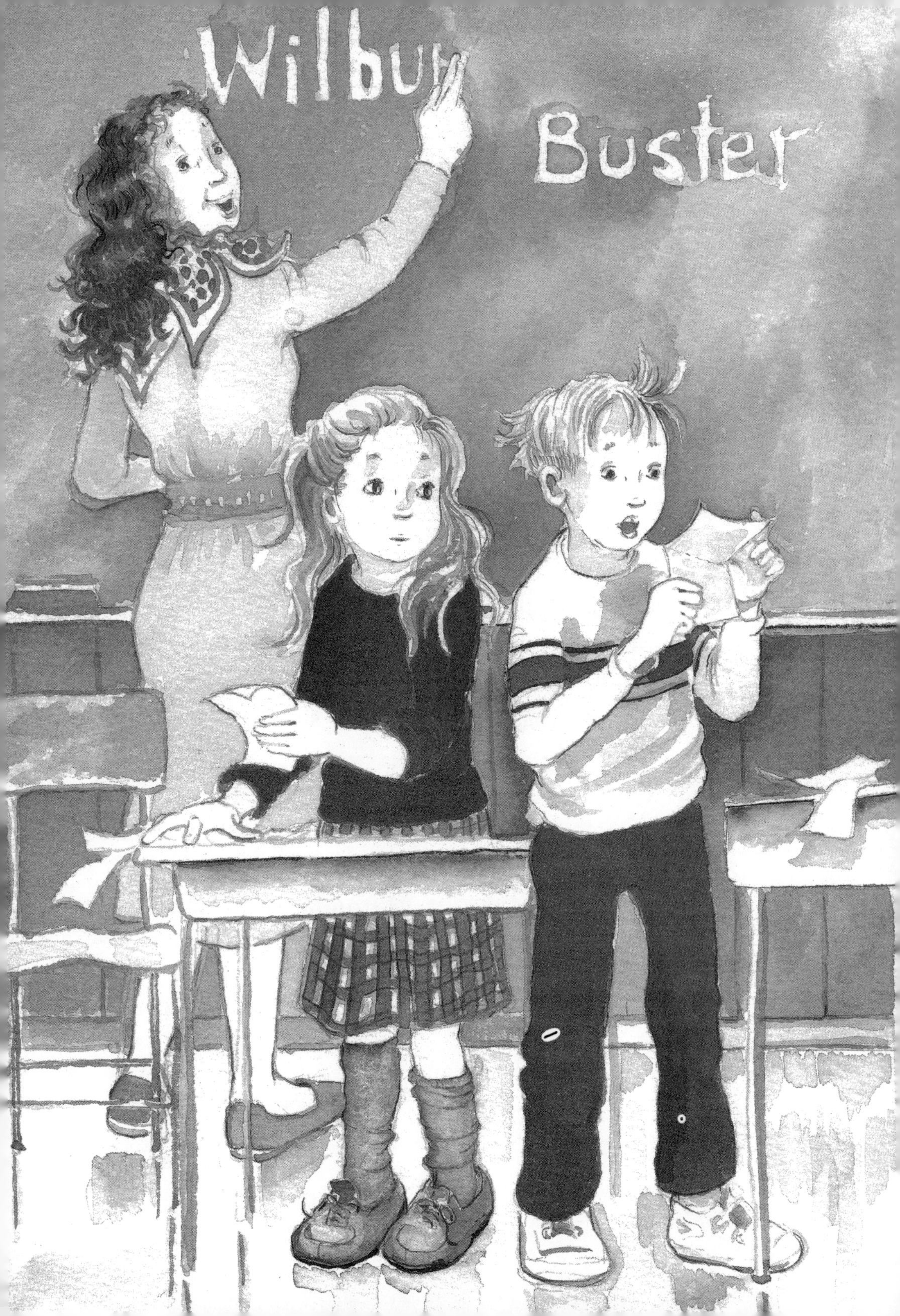
Wilbur
Buster

Quinn heard Manuela whisper, "That's mine!"

"It's my turn to read," interrupted Annie May.

"Go ahead, Annie May," said Mrs. Palmer, "you may read the last one."

Annie May looked at the paper.

"I don't know if I should," she said.

"Go ahead, Annie May." Mrs. Palmer sounded impatient.

"It says 'Manuela,'" said Annie May.

Quinn smiled at her new friend.

Manuela did not smile back. She looked like she might cry.

"That's mean," Annie May said to Quinn.

Manuela sniffled.

Quinn felt all mixed up. She thought Manuela was a beautiful name. And the pig was a beautiful pig. It had a beautiful smile. She thought Manuela would like the pig named after her. She thought that would make them best friends again.

"You didn't even spell it right," Annie

May said. "It's not M-a-n-y-u-e-l-l-a. It's M-A-N-U-E-L-A!"

Quinn stared hard at the top of her desk.

Mrs. Palmer clapped her hands. "Now, class, take out another piece of paper. Write down the name you like best."

"What if we don't know how to spell it?" Cody asked.

Mrs. Palmer pointed to the blackboard. "I wrote them all down for you. All you have to do is copy."

"Oh, yeah. I forgot." Cody dropped his pencil on the floor. "Sorry."

Pretty soon Mrs. Palmer collected all the pieces of paper. She sorted them into piles.

"Please take out your reading books and begin the story on page twenty-three while you are waiting."

Quinn opened her book.

She tried to catch Manuela's attention, but Manuela would not look up from her reading.

Quinn hid her face in her own book. The

45

words on the page were all wavy. Water blurred her eyes. She got up to get a tissue.

Jim waved his hand wildly. "You forgot to say what the prize was."

"I guess I did." Mrs. Palmer put down the papers. "If your name is picked, you may take our pig home for the evening."

Everyone cheered. Everyone except Quinn.

She had lost the contest. And, worst of all, she had lost her brand-new best friend.

CHAPTER EIGHT

Tiffany's name won.

"Yuck," said Jim. "What a baby name. Raspberry."

"Yeah," said Josh. "That's just because there are more girls in our class than boys. No boy would vote for it."

Cody grinned. "I did," he said.

"Oh, no," Jim and Josh said together, "how could you?"

"I liked it." Cody's cheeks turned pink.

Clap, clappa, clap, clap went Mrs. Palmer's hands.

Clap, clap, the children answered.

"It's time to get ready to go home, but the floor is too messy." Mrs. Palmer pointed at Jim and Josh. "Each person at the blue table needs to pick up five scraps and then they may go get their coats."

Quickly, children picked up scraps and got their mail from their mailboxes.

Quinn practically bumped into Manuela in the coatroom. But Manuela did not seem to notice. She did not even look at Quinn. She dropped her bookbag. Quinn picked it up and handed it to her.

"Manuela . . ." she started.

Suddenly, Annie May was there, pulling on Manuela's arm. "Come on, Tiffany's saving a place for us in the bus line."

"Hurry! Don't be late," Mrs. Palmer called. She brushed the last of the boys and girls out of the coatroom.

They lined up for the bus. Tiffany and Annie May stood on either side of Man-

uela. They all sat on the same seat when they got on.

Quinn sat by herself. It was a long ride.

Manuela got off with Tiffany and Annie May. Tiffany let Manuela carry Raspberry.

"What do you want to play when we get home?" Cody scooted back to sit with Quinn. He moved fast so that Dora, the bus driver, would not see him.

"You're not supposed to change seats," Quinn told him.

Cody held his bookbag tighter on his lap. "Nobody saw."

Quinn leaned her head against the window. "I don't know if I want to play after school."

"You don't?" Cody said. "But we were going to finish our fort."

Quinn bounced her legs against the seat.

"Don't you feel good?" asked Cody.

Quinn thought about it for a minute. Come to think of it, she did have a stomachache. "I might be catching something," she said.

"My mom said there are a lot of bugs around. Maybe one got on you."

"What kind of bugs?" Quinn asked. She pulled her hood up and tied it tight.

"Cold and flu bugs." Cody took off his baseball cap and fanned his face.

"You mean germs," said Quinn.

Cody put his cap back on. "They can still get you."

The bus stopped to let Cody, Quinn, and some of the other neighborhood children off.

Quinn moped all the way to her house.

"I'm home." She leaned against her mother's office door.

Mom looked up from her computer. "Why are you all bundled up? The sun is shining."

"I thought some bugs might get on me."

"Bugs?" Her mother watched Quinn hang up her jacket and bookbag.

"Not real bugs. Flu bugs and cold bugs."

"Are you feeling sick?" Mom looked confused. She felt Quinn's forehead.

"I do have a funny feeling in my stomach," said Quinn.

"Maybe you're hungry." She took Quinn's hand and they went into the kitchen.

Quinn looked in the refrigerator. "Tyson drank all the apple juice," she said.

Her mother sliced an orange. "Won't milk do?"

"I don't like milk. Especially not with oranges." Quinn felt around in the refrigerator. "Can I have this?" She pulled out a can of soda pop.

"Certainly not." Mom took the pop from Quinn and put it away.

52

"I'll just have water, then." Quinn sat down at the kitchen table.

She looked at the orange slices. She looked at the plain glass of water.

She put her head down on the table.

"You *aren't* feeling well, are you?" Her mother stroked Quinn's hair.

Quinn rocked her head back and forth on the table.

"Maybe what you need is a good rest."

Quinn wobbled her head from side to side. She did not think a rest would cure her bug. Orange slices and a glass of water would not cure her bug either.

She lifted her head off the table. "I don't think I should go to school tomorrow."

"Why?" asked her mother. "You don't have a fever."

"Because," Quinn said, flopping her head back down on her arms, "because I am allergic to pigs."

CHAPTER NINE

Tiffany was in the coatroom when Quinn got to school the next morning.

"Look what I did." She held the stuffed pig up for Quinn to see. "I found this ribbon in my grandma's sewing scraps. She said I could have it."

Now, instead of having a plain pink neck, Raspberry wore a green bow.

"That looks real nice," Quinn said.

"Feel it!" Tiffany held the pig out to her.

Quinn touched the ribbon. "It's so soft!"

"Velvet," said Tiffany. She hugged Raspberry close again. "I still can't believe my name won. I've never won anything in my life. Not even a birthday party game."

"I won a flashlight at the carnival last year," Quinn said, stroking Raspberry's soft head.

"Would you like to hold him?" Tiffany asked. "He makes you feel good. I even slept with him last night. I imagined he was really mine."

"I have a monkey named Chi-Chi," Quinn told her. It did feel good to hold Raspberry. "I sleep with him every night."

Tiffany flapped the sides of her coat like bird wings. "My grandma thinks I'm too old to sleep with stuffed animals."

Quinn thought about that. "How come?"

"I don't know." Tiffany dropped her arms to her sides. "It was sure nice sleeping with Raspberry."

Quinn handed the pig back.

"About the name contest—I know you didn't pick Manuela's name to be mean," said Tiffany.

That funny feeling started in Quinn's stomach again. "I didn't," Quinn said.

"Do you want me to tell her?" Tiffany wrapped Raspberry inside her coat.

"Okay." Quinn's stomach felt better. Tiffany was a good friend. "I'm glad your name won. Raspberry is a good name for our class pig."

"I hope Mrs. Palmer gives me another star today. For making a bow for Raspberry." Tiffany skipped a few steps. "What did you bring for the Pig Patch?"

The bell rang just then so Quinn didn't

have to answer. After Tiffany skipped away, Manuela came into the coatroom and hung up her things.

Quinn swallowed hard. Her stomach did tap dances. "Hi," she said.

Manuela looked at her. "Hi," she said back, very softly.

"Come on, Manuela." Annie May stood in the doorway. "I have something to show you."

Quinn stayed in the coatroom a long time after Manuela left. So long that Mrs. Palmer came looking for her.

"Are you all right?" she asked.

Quinn shrugged.

Mrs. Palmer touched Quinn's shoulder. "Would you do a special job for me?"

Quinn shrugged again.

"Go down to Mr. Crowell's room and ask if I can borrow back my tape player. It's kind of heavy. Do you think you can manage?"

Quinn nodded, but her insides got all wobbly. Mr. Crowell taught fourth grade.

He called kids by their last names and yelled at them if they did even one little twisty on the swings at recess. Every summer, all the third graders crossed their fingers against getting Mr. Crowell for a teacher.

Mr. Crowell was leading his class to music when Quinn arrived. He frowned when she delivered Mrs. Palmer's message.

"It's on the bookcase next to my desk," he said. "Go straight in and don't touch a thing."

Quinn swallowed but didn't answer. Mr. Crowell marched his class down the hall.

Quinn hurried straight into the classroom, afraid even to look around. She found the tape player, but as she pulled it off the shelf, several books tumbled off with it.

Quickly, she picked the books up and stuffed them back in the bookcase. One of the book covers caught her eye. A big fat pig was dancing.

She read the title. *Pigericks*. She opened

58

the book. It was a whole book of limericks about pigs!

It would be perfect for the Pig Patch! She would finally get her star. All she had to do was ask Mr. Crowell if she could borrow it.

That was all.

Quinn slowly put the book back on the shelf.

CHAPTER TEN

"Mrs. Palmer, Mrs. Palmer!" Annie May hurried into the classroom after the weekend. "Guess what Tiffany and I did!"

Quinn was at the rainbow work table, playing with the Unifix cubes. She stuck five black ones together to make a snake.

"I bet it's not as neat as what I get to do!" crowed Josh.

"Me first," said Annie May in her bossy voice.

"Yes, Annie May?" said Mrs. Palmer.

"Tiffany and I helped Manuela think of something for the Pig Patch. She's bringing it in right now." Annie May bustled over to the classroom door and held it open for Manuela.

"Whatever could be in that big sack?" Mrs. Palmer asked.

"A surprise." Manuela smiled. "Can I share it at lunchtime?"

Mrs. Palmer nodded.

"I have a surprise for the Pig Patch, too. Don't I, Mrs. Palmer?" Josh pushed his way between Annie May and Manuela. "My mom's friend is bringing in her pet pig today. A Vietnamese potbelly pig."

The class got so noisy and excited that Mrs. Palmer had to clap three times before things got quiet again. "Let's take our seats quickly, children. Manuela, why don't you put that sack under your desk?"

"Now, there's only *one* person who hasn't brought something for the Pig Patch," said Annie May, in a too-loud voice.

Quinn looked over at her, then crunched up the snake she'd been making. Ugly old Annie May snake.

There was a knock at the classroom door.

"It's Jelly Belly!" cried Josh. "He's here!"

"Seats, please, everyone." Mrs. Palmer gave instructions. "Jelly Belly is used to people, but his owner has asked that we try to be quiet and not crowd around."

Mrs. Palmer opened the classroom door and in walked Jelly Belly and his owner.

The children giggled when they saw his fat round stomach.

"Quietly, quietly," said Mrs. Palmer. "Josh, why don't you introduce our guests?"

"This is my friend Nancy and her pig, Jelly Belly. She lives near us and takes Jelly Belly

63

on a walk every day. He wears a leash and everything, just like now."

Nancy smiled. "He's a pretty good guy, but he'd run if I let him off the leash."

Royce's hand went up. "How old is he?"

"He's three months old and weighs 20 pounds. He'll get much bigger than he is now—maybe around 100 pounds."

"What does he like to eat?" asked Cody.

"He's wild about doughnuts. But he only gets them on Saturdays. I make him eat vegetables and other good things."

The children laughed.

Annie May waved her hand importantly. "I know a lot about pigs. My grandpa has some on his farm in North Dakota."

"That's great," said Nancy.

"Can we pet Jelly Belly?" asked Tiffany in a shy voice.

"May we," reminded Mrs. Palmer.

"How about if I walk him around the room? Pet him all you want but move slowly and talk quietly. He's not very happy

because he doesn't like riding in the car."
Nancy clucked to the pig softly, and he began to trot around the room.

His hair was wiry and rough. When Quinn petted him, he brushed his moist snout against her bare ankle. It made her shiver.

When he got to Annie May, Jelly Belly got very interested in the lace on her anklets. He started to nibble at it.

"Please," Annie May said quietly, "please get him away."

"I thought you knew all about pigs," said Jim, giggling at the faces Annie May was making.

"I know about my grandfather's pigs," Annie May said sharply. "Oh, he's going to eat me!" She jerked her leg away.

"He won't eat you," Nancy said. She tugged on Jelly Belly's collar. "Come on, boy."

The pig wouldn't budge. Quinn could see he had his heart set on Annie May's socks.

"P-p-please get him away," begged Annie May.

"Here, pig." Nancy yanked harder.

Just then, Jelly Belly got a good grip on Annie May's lace sock. When Nancy pulled him, he pulled Annie May.

"HELPPPP!" screamed Annie May. "He's eating me!"

"EEEE," squealed Jelly Belly. He bucked up under Annie May's desk. It crashed to the floor. Jelly Belly twisted around, jerking the leash out of Nancy's hands. He snorted and started to run.

Kids screamed and leaped out of the way. Jelly Belly scrambled this way and that across the slick linoleum floor.

"Calm down, children!" shouted Mrs. Palmer.

"Whoa, there, Jelly Belly!" shouted Nancy.

"He's got me!" shouted Royce. Jelly Belly had turned a corner and wrapped his leash around Royce's legs.

Quinn stood frozen by her desk. Nancy dived for the leash and missed it. Jelly Belly knocked over the rainbow table and sent Unifix cubes flying.

Children were climbing on desks and counters to get out of the way of the frightened pig. Annie May didn't stop screaming the whole time.

It seemed more like a circus than a classroom.

"Down, pig!" called Nancy.

"Mama!" moaned Annie May.

"Oh, my goodness," said Mrs. Palmer.

Jelly Belly was headed straight for Manuela's desk. Manuela jumped aside just as Jelly Belly dove through the table legs. A huge POP exploded in the room, surprising everyone, including Jelly Belly. The noise stopped him long enough for Nancy to grab hold of his leash.

"My pig!" said Manuela. She picked up the bag Jelly Belly had trampled. She pulled out a squashed pink mess. Even

though it was smashed, Quinn could tell it had been a balloon decorated to look like a pig.

"It's ruined," Manuela said in a small, tight voice.

"I think Jelly Belly and I will be on our way," said Nancy. She dragged the pig out the door.

"Maybe Nancy could bring Jelly Belly back another day," said Josh.

"One visit is probably enough," said Mrs. Palmer. "Okay, children, let's start picking up the room."

Manuela sniffled as she threw her pig balloon in the garbage. Quinn helped her turn her desk right side up.

Manuela started to pick up her pencil box, then she just sat down. She put her head down on her desk.

She kept it down for a very long time.

CHAPTER ELEVEN

Quinn could not get Manuela's sad face out of her mind all day.

During math, instead of subtracting, she stared at the Pig Patch chart. Two holes, just like in Manuela's smile. One for Manuela and one for Quinn.

When everyone else was doing penmanship, Quinn wrote Manuela a note. "I know how you feel," it said.

But Quinn threw it away. She was afraid

that Manuela would not read anything from her, not even a cheer-up note.

Quinn hardly realized when it was time for lunch. It was the "cook's choice"—pigs in a blanket. She thought she'd go crazy.

Tiffany, Annie May, and Manuela finished their lunches quickly and went out to recess. Quinn sat on the monkey bars and watched them. Tiffany and Annie May tried to get Manuela to do double Dutch.

Manuela sat on the bench watching. Even from the monkey bars, Quinn could see her hunched shoulders and long face.

Quinn hung by her knees. She liked being upside down. It gave her a fresh look at things. Upside down, Manuela wore a smile. That made Quinn feel a little better.

Now, Annie May and Tiffany were trying to get Manuela to play four square. Quinn wished she were with them. She was sure she would know how to cheer Manuela up. Friends can do that for each other.

"Girls, girls," Mr. Crowell called to some fifth graders on the swings, "no twisties. I've told you several times. Shall I send you to Mrs. Moore and have her explain the rules?"

The girls stopped twisting, but one stuck her tongue out at Mr. Crowell as he walked away.

Mr. Crowell. The *Pigericks* book.

Without giving herself a chance to think about it, Quinn jumped off the monkey bars and hurried after him.

"Mr. Crowell!" she called, walking as fast as she could. She didn't want to get in trouble with him for running.

"Yes?" He stopped and turned around. "Oh, hello," he said when he recognized Quinn.

Quinn tried to say something, but her mouth felt like it had been in a freezer.

"Is something wrong?" Mr. Crowell asked.

"No. Yes." Quinn shook her head. "I mean, I need to ask you a favor."

"Me?" Mr. Crowell took the whistle from his mouth.

Quinn took a deep breath and dived right in. As fast as she could talk, she told Mr. Crowell about National Pig Day and the Pig Patch chart and the stars. She took another deep breath when she finished.

"Hmmm," was all Mr. Crowell said. "Now why are you telling me all this?"

"I was wondering if I could borrow— just borrow, and I'd take very good care of it—the *Pigericks* book for our Pig Patch."

Mr. Crowell cleared his throat. "I don't usually lend my books to students."

Quinn wasn't quick enough to stop the tear that formed in her eye. She blinked and started to turn away.

"However," said Mr. Crowell, "if you

promise that it will remain in the class-room, I will make an exception. Just this once."

Quinn's feet did a skip-hop and so did her heart. "Oh, thank you! Thank you so much."

"Why don't you come with me now and we'll get it?"

When Mr. Crowell handed her the book, Quinn almost thought she saw a twinkle in his eye.

She still hoped she didn't get him for fourth grade.

CHAPTER TWELVE

Quinn hurried to be the first one in her seat after recess. She held up her library book and acted like she was reading. She kept one eye on Manuela's desk.

Finally, Manuela came in. She picked up the note Quinn had left her. She looked around, then bent over and looked in her desk. She smiled when she saw the book.

"Where did you get this?" she asked Quinn.

"I borrowed it," Quinn answered. "It's for you. To put in the Pig Patch."

"But then you'll be the only one without a star."

Quinn straightened the things on her desk. "It doesn't matter."

Manuela smiled her beautiful permanent teeth smile.

"I'm sorry for hurting your feelings," said Quinn. "I think Manuela is a beautiful name. I think the pig is a beautiful pig. I thought it would fit perfectly."

"You think Manuela is a beautiful name?"

Quinn nodded.

"I hate it."

"You do?"

"I want to change my name. To Jessica. Or maybe Diane. My mother says I can't until I'm eighteen."

Quinn never would have guessed that Manuela didn't like her beautiful name. She wished she had known that. Friends should tell each other things.

Suddenly, Quinn remembered. "I am sorry I didn't call you the other day. I wanted to come over to your house, but I had a dentist appointment. I didn't think you'd believe me about the appointment."

"You didn't?"

"I thought you might think I was making an excuse. That I didn't really want to come over."

"I thought you didn't like me, after all," said Manuela.

"I guess sometimes even friends can have mix-ups."

"I guess so." Manuela picked up the *Pigericks* book. "How about if you come over on Friday?"

"I'll ask my mom and call you tonight." Quinn crossed her heart. "I promise."

"Know what else?"

"What?" asked Quinn.

"I like to be called Lolly."

"Okay, Lolly." Quinn thought for a minute. "I still like Manuela best. But Lolly is good, too."

"That's what my mother says," said Manuela.

CHAPTER THIRTEEN

Quinn raced to the phone as soon as she got home from school.

"My mother says Friday is okay!"

"Oh, that's so great!" Manuela giggled. "Guess what else is great?"

"I don't know. I'm not a good guesser," said Quinn.

"I thought of something for the Pig Patch."

"But you have the book," said Quinn, confused.

"Yes, but this is something from us both together." Manuela told Quinn her plan. Quinn got a piece of paper and pencil. She laughed as she wrote down Manuela's plan and filled up the paper with words and cross-outs.

"The phone is not a toy," Quinn's mother called from her office.

"I have to go," Quinn said.

"I'll see you tomorrow, Quinny," said Manuela.

"I'll see you tomorrow, Lolly." Quinn laughed again.

"Quinn!" Her mother's voice was sharp.

"Bye," Quinn said quickly, then hung up the phone.

She did a dance around the kitchen. Shuffle-hop, shuffle-hop. Just like she learned in tap-dance class.

She grabbed a red marker and put a big circle around Friday on the calendar. She drew a fat *M* in the square. A red *M* for Manuela day. She could hardly wait.

CHAPTER FOURTEEN

Mrs. Palmer clapped her hands. Clap, clappa, clap, clap.

The children answered. Clap, clap.

"We have something very special for the Pig Patch. Quinn, Manuela, will you come forward?"

Quinn giggled.

The girls walked to the front of the room. Each held one end of a piece of paper.

Manuela giggled.

"We're ready, girls," Mrs. Palmer said.

84

Quinn dropped her end of the paper. She grabbed it back again.

" 'Our Pigerick'," said Manuela and Quinn, together.

"There once were two piggly friends,
Their friendship went on without end.
These pigs, Quinn and Lolly,
  took a ride on a trolley.
Those two very piggly friends."

The girls took a bow. Everybody clapped.

"What a wonderful rhyme!" Mrs. Palmer clapped, too.

Quinn showed her the book. Mrs. Palmer read it to the whole class. She wore a big smile when she finished.

She put the book right in the very middle of the Pig Patch shelf.

"This gives me an idea," Mrs. Palmer said. "Would anyone else like to write pigericks?"

Everyone put thumbs up.

Quinn sat up very straight and looked over at Manuela. Manuela smiled her filled-in smile. Quinn smiled back with her holey smile.

Everyone got busy working on pigericks. Jim and Josh and Cody worked together.

"Quiet voices," Mrs. Palmer reminded them.

"We forgot," said Cody.

"This is so much fun, I'm going to do it every year," said Mrs. Palmer.

Quinn walked over to look at the Pig Patch chart. Mrs. Palmer had pasted extra-big gold stars where it said QUINN and where it said MANUELA.

Quinn skipped back to her seat.

Second grade was pig-perfect!

Cody ————————— ☆
Tiffany ————————— ☆
Josh ————————— ☆
Annie May ————————— ☆
Quinn ————————— ★
Jim ————————— ☆
Royce ————————— ☆
Manuela ————————— ☆